I love
Pennsylvania
an ABC adventure

Sandra Magsamen

Pennsylvania is filled with fantastic and beautiful things to see and do. Just follow the **A, B, C's,** there is an amazing adventure waiting for you!

The Keystone State

Erie

Williamsport

Scranton

New Castle

Allentown

Pittsburgh

Harrisburg

Lancaster

Philadelphia

Gettysburg

A

is for the **Appalachian Trail.** Take an awesome hiking vacation!

B is for the Liberty **Bell**. It rings for our one-of-a-kind nation.

liberty

C is for celebrating our cuisine.

We're famous for yummy pretzels, cheesesteaks and shoo-fly pie.

D is for the **Declaration of Independence,** signed in Philadelphia on the Fourth of July.

life, liberty and the pursuit of happiness

F is for fireflies.

Our state insect is full of zest!

H is for **Hersheypark.** The roller coasters here are thrilling— they're the best!

I is for Italian ice. It's a cool and tasty treat!

J
is for
jumping
into Lake
Wallenpaupack
to beat
the
heat.

K

is for
kayaking
the

Susquehanna
to the
Chesapeake Bay.

L

is for **Lancaster,**
where Amish
families
live, work
and play.

M is for museums.
We've got them all!

From art to history, they are really cool!

Franklin Institute

Andy Warhol Museum

Children's Museum of Pittsburgh

Railroad Museum

Ben Franklin Museum

N

is for

nibbling

on

fasnachts.

These sugary doughnuts will surely make you drool!

O

is for
**Ohiopyle
State Park.**

Come raft
down a
waterfall.

R

is for the **Ruffled Grouse.** Our state bird is quite the feathered sight!

S

is for the **Steelers.** Fans love to wave their "terrible towels" in the air.

terrible towel

T is for **touch** at the Please Touch Museum. Take a trip and touch, play and share!

U is for the United States.

Our first flag was made in Philadelphia by Betsy Ross.

V is for the **varmint** known as Punxsutawney Phil. He's our cute and handsome weather boss.

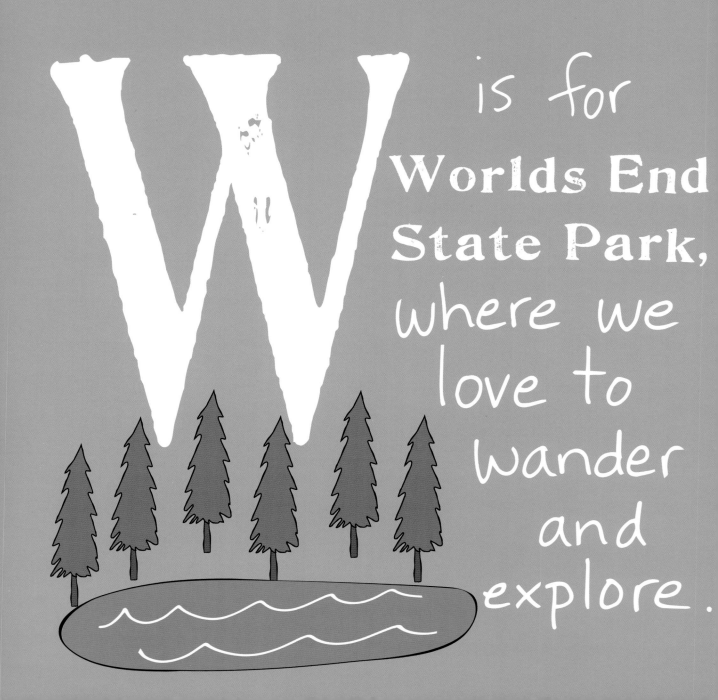

W is for **Worlds End State Park,** where we love to wander and explore.

Y is for York.

This really beautiful town is also known as the White Rose City.

adventure

an end,
can go
A and
again!

life,
liberty
and the
pursuit
of
happiness

Sandra Magsamen is a best-selling and award-winning artist, author, and designer whose meaningful and message-driven art has touched millions of lives, one heart at a time. She loves to travel and has had many awesome adventures around the world. For now, she lives happily and artfully in Vermont with her family and their dog, Olive.

A big thank you to my amazing studio team of Hannah Barry and Karen Botti. Their creativity, research tenacity and spirit of adventure have been invaluable as we crafted the ABC adventure series.

Sandra Magsamen

Text and illustrations © 2016 Hanny Girl Productions, Inc. www.sandramagsamen.com
Exclusively represented by Mixed Media Group, Inc. NY, NY.
Cover and internal design © 2016 by Sandra Magsamen

Published by Sourcebooks Jabberwocky, an imprint of Sourcebooks, Inc.
P.O. Box 4410, Naperville, Illinois 60567-4410
(630) 961-3900
Fax: (630) 961-2168
www.sourcebooks.com

Library of Congress Cataloging-in-Publication data is on file with the publisher.

Source of Production: Leo Paper, Heshan City, Guangdong Province, China
Date of Production: June 2016
Run Number: 5006252

Printed and bound in China.
LEO 10 9 8 7 6 5 4 3 2 1

The Keystone State

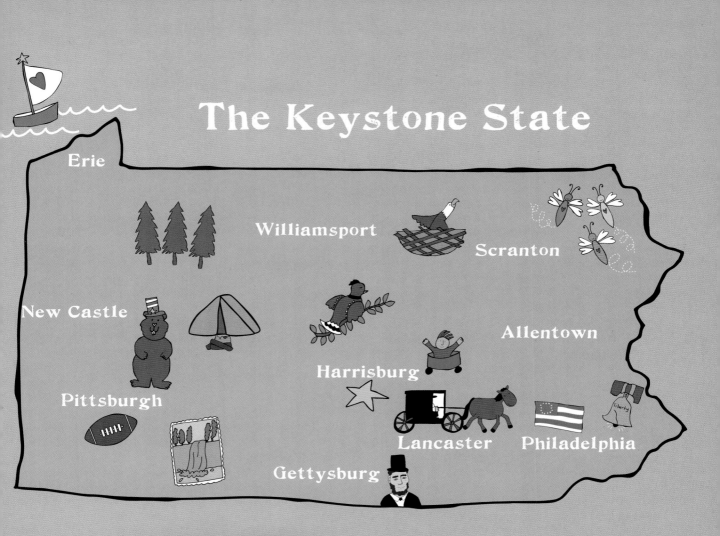

Erie

Williamsport

Scranton

New Castle

Allentown

Harrisburg

Pittsburgh

Lancaster

Philadelphia

Gettysburg